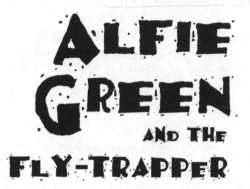

ALFIE GREEN

AND THE FLY-TRAPPER

Joe O'Brien

Illustrated by Jean Texier

THE O'BRIEN PRESS
DUBLIN

First published 2006 by The O'Brien Press Ltd.,
12 Terenure Road East, Rathgar, Dublin 6, Ireland.
Tel: +353 1 4923333; Fax: +353 1 4922777
E-mail: books@obrien.ie
Website: www.obrien.ie

ISBN-10: 0-86278-954-0
ISBN-13: 978-0-86278-954-1

British Library Cataloguing-in-Publication Data
O'Brien, Joe
Alfie Green and the fly-trapper
1. Green, Alfie (Fictitious character) - Juvenile fiction
2. Magic - Juvenile fiction 3. Children's stories
I. Title II. Texier, Jean
823.9'2[J]

2 3 4 5 6 7 8 9 10
06 07 08 09 10

The O'Brien Press receives
assistance from

the arts
council
schomhairle
ealaíon

Editing, typesetting, layout, design: The O'Brien Press Ltd.
Illustrations: Jean Texier
Printing: Reálszisztéma Dabas Printing House, Hungary

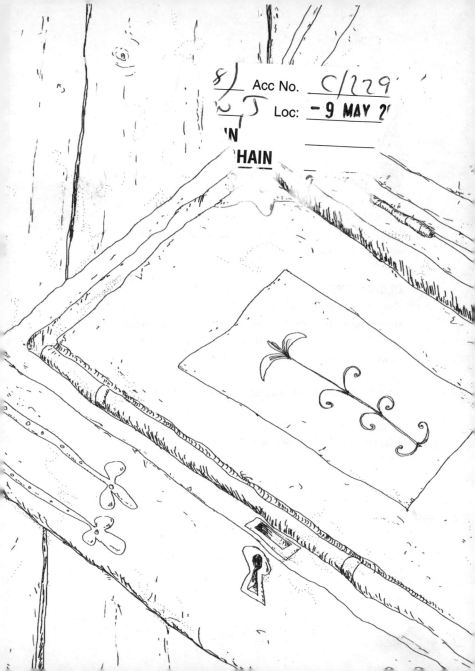

JOE O'BRIEN is an award-winning gardener who lives in Ballyfermot in Dublin. This is his fourth book about the wonderful world of Alfie Green.

DEDICATION

The *Alfie Green* series is dedicated to my son, Ethan, who in his short time in this world taught me to be strong, happy and thankful for the gift of life. Thank you, Ethan, for the inspiration to write.

Alfie Green and the Fly-Trapper is dedicated to my dear late Mam.

ACKNOWLEDGEMENTS:
A big thank you to all at The O'Brien Press, to Jean Texier, and, of course, to my readers.

*　　　*　　　*

JEAN TEXIER is a storyboard artist and illustrator. Initially trained in animation, he has worked in the film industry for many years.

CONTENTS

CHAPTER 1

THERE'S A BIRD IN THE HOUSE!

'He's coming!' Alfie Green hopped off the chair and shut the window as he spotted his brother Bobby passing Mrs Butler's gate.

'Has he caught anything?' his dad asked.

'If you saw the look on his face, you wouldn't ask,' Alfie replied.

Every Sunday, Bobby Green set off
for the river with his fishing rod and a
tub of maggots. Every Sunday he
came back without a fish.

Alfie gave his dad a thumbs-up as he heard Bobby turn the key in the door.

'A one, a two, a three,' said his dad, and Alfie and Lucy joined in as he sang:

'ALWAYS LOOK ON THE BRIGHT SIDE OF LIFE.'

'Oh, very funny, ha ha,' Bobby said, and he walked into the kitchen.

'Don't leave that tub of maggots on the fridge.' Alfie's mother warned. 'They're **disgusting**.'

' I'll move them in a minute, Mam,' Bobby said. 'Let me bring my fishing gear out back first.'

Just then there was a flapping
noise. A magpie had seen the
maggots through the open window.

**'THERE'S A BIRD IN THE
HOUSE,'** Alfie's mother screamed.

The poor bird got such a fright that he knocked the tub of maggots down the back of the fridge.

Then he flew round and round the kitchen, trying to find a way out.

Alfie, Lucy and Bobby chased the bird towards the window.

'**Mind the clock!** Watch out for the trifle ...' Alfie's mother yelled.

CRASH! The glass bowl with Granny's special Sunday trifle smashed onto the tiled floor. The trifle went **EVERYWHERE**.

The crazed bird flew out of the
window, leaving the kitchen covered
in big blobs of cream, yellow custard
and orange jelly.

It took a whole hour to clean up the mess. The dinner was burnt. And there was NO DESSERT.

And in all the fuss, everyone **forgot** about the tub of maggots.

Oh dear!

CHAPTER 2

FLIES

A week later, Alfie was coming home from school when he saw Doctor Power's car driving away from his house.

'What's happened?' he asked his dad.

'Shush, Alfie,' said Mr Green. 'Granny's sick and she's trying to sleep.'

'What's wrong with her?'

'Flies,' said his dad.

'FLIES??'

Alfie's dad brought him out to the kitchen. It was full of flies.

'Wow!' said Alfie. 'Where did they come from?'

Alfie's dad told him how Granny had gone to the fridge to get milk for her porridge. When she banged the door shut, a big cloud of flies flew up from behind the fridge and whizzed around her head.

Poor Granny had run screeching to her bedroom and refused to come out.

'But where did the flies come from?' Alfie asked. 'Oh – Bobby's maggots!'

'Spot on, Alfie,' said his dad. 'Maggots turn into flies.'

Alfie had an idea. 'Dad, I've got a small plant on my bedroom window that catches flies. It's called a Venus Fly-Trap. Maybe that can help?'

'Good man, Alfie,' said his dad, 'Let's give it a try.'

Alfie's fly-trapper did its best, but there were just too many flies. Soon the little plant was full.

'Blaagh,'

it burped.
'I think I'm going to be sick.'

Time for some magic, Alfie thought. He took his fly-trapper out to the shed to see the wise old plant.

CHAPTER 3

A GIANT FLY-TRAPPER

Alfie took the magical book from under the floorboards. He put his hand on the seed on the first page. The wise old plant rose up from the page until it towered over Alfie.

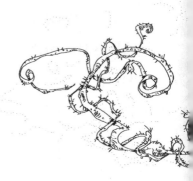

'Another problem, Alfie?' asked the

wise old plant.

Alfie told him about the flies.

'Well, I'm afraid your fly-trapper isn't big enough for this job,' said the wise old plant. 'Just look at him – he's stuffed.'

'What can I do?' Alfie asked.

The wise old plant flicked through the magical book until he came to a page that said 'Giant Fly-Trapper'.

'Wow!' Alfie was gobsmacked.

The Giant Fly-Trapper had eight heads filled with razor-sharp teeth. The heads swivelled from side to side, snapping up flies in big mouthfuls.

'I wish *my* plant was a Giant
Fly-Trapper,' said Alfie.

The wise old plant plucked a blue hair from its leaves and dropped it into the small plant's mouth.

Nothing happened for a second. Then the plant shot up, grew three more heads and burst out of its plastic pot. It looked very pleased with itself.

'Wicked!' said Alfie. 'Is it a Giant Fly-Trapper now?'

'Not quite,' answered the wise old plant. 'A *real* Giant Fly-Trapper would cause terrible trouble in your world, Alfie. But he could turn into one if you don't obey one very important rule.'

'What rule?' asked Alfie.

'Don't feed him anything except flies!'

And then the book closed with a

SLAM!

CHAPTER 4

SNAPPER

Alfie put his new fly-trapper into a bigger pot.

'I think I'll call you Snapper,' he said. He brought the pot into the kitchen and sat it on top of the fridge.

SNAP ... cRUNCh ... MuNCh ... cHOMp ... GuLP ...

Soon Snapper had gobbled up every fly in the house.

Alfie knocked on Granny's bedroom door. 'You can come out now, Gran,' he shouted. 'The flies are gone.'

Granny thought Alfie was a real hero. She gave him money to get ice cream.

Lucy met Alfie at the door when he got back from the shops. She was carrying her rabbits, Posh and Becks.

'Guess what, Alfie,' said Lucy.

'What?' asked Alfie, licking the last of the chocolate ice cream from around his mouth.

'Snapper likes carrots.'

'Carrots ... You fed **carrots** to Snapper?'

Alfie remembered the wise old plant's warning.

He ran into the kitchen and
stopped in shock.

Snapper was bursting
out of his new pot.
His heads were
twice as big as
before!

Alfie knew
how cross the
wise old plant
would be. He
decided to fix
this himself.

If I give him lots of exercise and don't feed him, maybe he'll shrink, he thought.

Alfie got Bobby to help him tie Snapper on to his skateboard with two bicycle straps.

Once he got up some speed, he put
both feet on the skateboard and held
on tight to Snapper.

'Wheeeeeeeee,' they sped up and down Alfie's road like a rocket.

'Way to go, Alfie,' yelled Fitzer as Alfie and Snapper whizzed by.

CHAPTER 5

THE TAIL OF A CAT

Alfie put Snapper in the back garden the next morning, but when he got home from school he found an even BIGGER Snapper on a three-wheeled, buckled skateboard.

Sticking out of three of Snapper's mouths were a bicycle tyre, a watering can ... and **THE TAIL OF A CAT**.

Snapper had turned into a Giant Fly-Trapper! Now he would eat anything.

The wise old plant was very cross
when he saw Snapper.

'I warned you not to feed that plant.'

'It wasn't me,' Alfie said. 'It was Lu–'

'You were in charge, Alfie,' the wise old plant said sternly. 'Now, what are we going to do?'

'I wonder if he'd be happy in Arcania?' asked Alfie.

'Hmm!' said the wise old plant, turning over the pages of the magical book, 'There **is** somewhere there that might suit him: the Belching Bogs. It's where all the insect-eating plants live.'

A horrible smell and very rude noises came out of the book.

'Uugh! That's disgusting,' Alfie said, holding his nose. 'It reminds me of the evil swamp.'

'That's because it's **in** the swamp,' the wise old plant said, smiling at the horrified look on Alfie's face.

'No way! I'm not going through the swamp again!'

'All right, all right, Alfie,' the wise old plant said. 'Go and get your crystal orchid and I'll think of some other way.'

Alfie took his crystal orchid out of the biscuit tin and put it in his pocket.

'I'm ready,' he announced.

'Right,' said the wise old plant, 'I've found a shortcut through the Nanabur Mines. Your Arcanian friends will know the way.

'And you can untie Snapper from that thing,' he added. 'Once the door to Arcania opens, he will be able to walk by himself.'

Then he folded himself back into

the book, which closed with a

CHAPTER 6

LOOK BEHIND YOU!

'Lads! I'm back,' Alfie called out as he and Snapper stepped from the shed into Arcania.

Jimmy the clippers bladed out of the high grass. Then he saw Snapper.

Jimmy stopped so suddenly that Paddy the spade, Mick the hoe and Vinny the fork crashed into him.

'Alfie, run! There's a THING behind you!' Jimmy yelled.

'Uh-oh,' said Paddy. 'A Giant Fly-Trapper!'

Alfie laughed. 'It's all right, Snapper's a friend.'

The four tools slowly headed over towards Snapper for a closer look.

Suddenly one of Snapper's razor-filled heads swivelled around towards them.

'BOO!'

Paddy, Jimmy, Mick and Vinny leapt with fright.

Snapper thought this was very funny and every one of his heads started laughing.

'Behave yourself, Snapper,' Alfie told him. 'Or my friends won't take us to the Nanabur Mines.'

'The Nanabur Mines?' Mick looked worried. 'You can't go through the Nanabur Mines.'

'Why not?' Alfie asked.

'Because they're full of Nanaburs,' said Vinny.

'Would somebody please tell me what a Nanabur is?' asked Alfie.

'Nanaburs,' said Paddy, 'have round prickly heads with snouts like pigs. They have beady eyes that glow in the dark. Their legs are stumpy and woody, and their teeth are rotten and smell of dead bugs.'

'Yes,' said Jimmy. 'And they spend most of their time mining for Blubber Bugs to stuff their horrid faces.'

'Yeucch!' Alfie said. 'I wouldn't like to meet one of them. But I **have** to take Snapper to the Belching Bogs. So we'd better get going.'

CHAPTER 7

THE NANABUR MINES

As they walked along, Alfie told Snapper about his other adventures in Arcania.

Jimmy had been scouting ahead. He called out, 'Over here!'

'This is as far as we can go, Alfie,' Paddy said. 'Nanaburs are always on the look-out for tools to use as slaves in their mines. Sorry.'

'What's that?' Mick pointed to a sign over the entrance to the mine.

'It looks like a warning,' Alfie said.
'But I don't understand the words.'

'It's written in Arcanum,' Paddy
said. 'Tools can't read Arcanum.'

'But plants can,' Snapper said proudly. He began to read out loud:

> **All Nanaburs BEWARE.**
> **This mine is now home to the**
> **deadly mine monster.**
> **DO NOT ENTER!**

'You're kidding!' Alfie said. 'First it was smelly Nanaburs and now it's a deadly mine monster. That's it, I'm not going in.'

'Good decision, Alfie,' Vinny nodded.

'Very wise, Alfie,' Paddy agreed.

Snapper said nothing, but all of his heads drooped and it seemed to Alfie that he shrank a little.

'What am I saying?' Alfie cried. 'Of course I can go in there. Haven't I got a Giant Fly-Trapper to protect me?'

Snapper's heads shot up, he bared his razor-sharp teeth and looked very fierce.

'See,' Alfie said to the tools. 'That old mine monster won't stand a chance!'

Paddy didn't look very happy.

'Well, if you're sure, Alfie ...'

'Of course I'm sure,' Alfie said. 'We'll be fine!'

He waved goodbye to his pals and stepped into the mine.

CHAPTER 8

WORMS

It was very cold in the mine, and very, very dark. Alfie and Snapper kept bumping into walls and tripping over cracks in the ground.

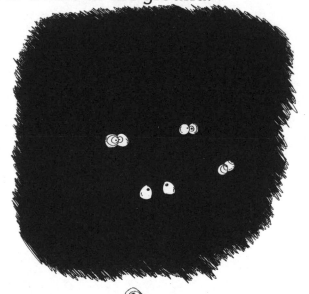

Then Alfie had an idea. 'We can use the crystal orchid as a light!'

He took the glass flower from his pocket. 'If you hold it up high, Snapper, we'll be able to see where we're going.'

Snapper held the shining flower between his teeth and it lit up the path ahead.

'That's better,' said Alfie. 'Now we can move faster.'

Alfie and Snapper walked for a long time through small tunnels and big caves without seeing any sign of a monster or a Nanabur.

'Maybe there's no monster at all, Snapper,' Alfie said. 'Maybe it's just a trick to keep the Nanaburs out?'

Snapper wasn't listening. It was a long time since his last meal and he had just seen a big juicy bug go past.

He charged after the whizzing bug.

The light from the crystal orchid waved all around the walls of the mine as Snapper swivelled his heads to catch his meal.

'**STOP**, Snapper,' shouted Alfie. 'I can't see where I'm going.'

Snapper stretched out to grab the bug. Just as he was about to SNAP, he fell into a huge hole in the floor.

Poor Alfie couldn't stop himself in time. He fell right in after Snapper.

'**Aghhhhhhhhhhhh,**' he screamed as he fell, down, down, down.

SQUELCH! Alfie landed flat on his back on something soft and squishy and ... and ... MOVING!

'Snapper,' he gasped, trying to get his breath back. 'DON'T MOVE, but shine the light on my legs.'

Fat, brown, slimy, squirmy worms wriggled under Alfie knees and hands. He could feel one crawling in his HAIR! They had fallen into a huge worm pit.

CHAPTER 9

THE DEADLY MINE MONSTER

Alfie was afraid to yell in case one of the worms got in his mouth.

Snapper was delighted. It was like falling into a five-star restaurant where he could eat EVERYTHING on the menu.

He reached out to fill his heads with delicious juicy worms.

Suddenly there was a **WHOOSH**

and an **enorMOUS** worm, as tall as
two houses, rose up out of the pit.

'The deadly mine monster!' Alfie yelled.

THUMP! The monster knocked Snapper right out of the worm pit and up against a wall.

'Stop!' Alfie shouted bravely. The monster's head turned towards the noise. She slithered down until her face was close to Alfie's. Her mouth opened.

Snapper charged off the edge of the path and jumped on to the monster, biting into her thick leathery skin with his sharp teeth.

With a roar, the monster flung herself back at Snapper and swung him in the air. The brave fly-trapper held on tight, like a cowboy riding a wild horse in a rodeo.

This was Alfie's chance. He grabbed at roots of branches and bits of rock and hauled himself up to the edge of the pit.

Out of the darkness something grasped his hand and pulled him to safety.

Alfie looked up to thank his rescuer. It was a Nanabur!

The Nanabur smiled at Alfie, grinding its rotten teeth. A boy would make a fine meal.

The Nanabur grabbed Alfie's leg and was just about to drag him into the darkness when ... **BANG!**

Snapper had lost his grip of the monster and came crashing into the Nanabur, knocking him sideways into the worm pit.

The worm monster lunged at the screeching Nanabur.

Alfie and Snapper raced through the mine, never stopping until they saw a light up ahead.

'Daylight!' Alfie shouted.

They climbed the rocky slope out of the mine to the top of a small hill and sat there, gasping.

'That was a close shave, Snapper,' Alfie said. 'I hope you still have the crystal orchid.'

'Right here, Alfie,' Snapper unfolded one of his heads, and there, safe and sound, was the orchid.

They stumbled down the other side of the hill. The ground became wet and bouncy under their feet.

'Phew!' Alfie said. 'What a pong!'

BURP, BLAAGH, YEEAGH ... A huge belching noise was followed by another and another. They had reached the Belching Bogs.

CHAPTER 10

THE BELCHING BOGS

'Home!' Snapper said happily. He could see lots of Giant Fly-Trappers in the distance.

I'm glad it's not MY home, Alfie thought.

'You'd better not go any further, Alfie,' Snapper advised. 'Some of those plants don't look very boy-friendly.'

The way ahead was carpeted with Sticky Sundews, Giant Pitchers and other carniverous plants.

'Goodbye, Alfie.' Snapper leaned over and hugged all of his long necks around Alfie.

Alfie took the crystal orchid from Snapper and grasped it with both hands. There was a flash of blinding light and Alfie was back in his grandad's shed.

He put the orchid away, picked up the skateboard and locked the shed door behind him.

'**ALFIE!**' his mother yelled from the house. 'Mrs Pearse is here to see you ... with her CAT!'

YIKES! I knew I recognised that tail, thought Alfie as he raced around to the side gate.

'Thanks a lot, Snapper,' he said out loud. 'Now I have Mad Aggie Pearse after me. And that's nearly as bad as a Nanabur!'

Then he made a wobbly but quick getaway out the gate.

READ ALFIE'S OTHER GREAT ADVENTURES IN:

Belching Bogs

The Croo...

Valley

The Swamp

Firethorn

Honeycomb
Mountain

ARCA

Sleepy Meadows

Nanabus
Mines

Alfie's
House

BUDSVILLE AVENUE